THE FIRST BOOK OF BARITONE/BASS SOLOS

PART II

compiled by Joan Frey Boytim

ISBN 0-7935-2497-0

G. SCHIRMER, Inc.

Distributed by
Hal Leonard Publishing Corporation
7777 West Bluemound Road P.O. Box 13819 Milwaukee, WI 53213

PREFACE

The widespread acceptance by teachers and students of "The First Book Series" for Soprano, Mezzo-Soprano/Alto, Tenor, Baritone/Bass has prompted the development of a Part II addition for each voice type. After discussions with numerous voice teachers, the key suggestion expressed many times was that there is a need for "more of the same" type of literature at exactly the same level.

The volumes in Part II follow many of the same concepts which are covered in the Preface of the original volumes, including a comprehensive selection of between 34 and 37 songs from the Baroque through the 20th Century. The selections range from easy to moderate difficulty for both singer and accompanist.

In response to many requests, we have included more sacred songs, and have added two Christmas solos in each volume. The recommendation for more humorous songs for each voice was honored as well.

Even though these books have a heavy concentration of English and American songs, we have also expanded the number of Italian, German, and French offerings. For those using the English singing translations, we have tried to find the translations that are most singable, and in several cases have reworked the texts.

Part II can easily stand alone as a first book for a beginning high school, college, or adult student. Because of the varied contents, Part II can also be successfully used in combination with the first volume of the series for an individual singer. This will give many choices of vocal literature, allowing for individual differences in student personality, maturity, and musical development.

Hal Leonard Publishing (distributor of G. Schirmer) and Richard Walters, supervising editor, have been most generous in allowing the initial objective for this series to be expanded more fully through publishing these companion volumes. We hope this new set of books will provide yet another interesting and exciting new source of repertoire for both the teacher and student.

Joan Frey Boytim
September, 1993

About the Compiler...

Since 1968, Joan Frey Boytim has owned and operated a full-time voice studio in Carlisle, Pennsylvania, where she has specialized in developing a serious and comprehensive curriculum and approach to teaching and coaching adolescent and community adult students. Her teaching experience has also included music and choral instruction at the junior high and senior high levels, and voice instruction at the college level. She is the author of a widely used bibliography, *Solo Vocal Repertoire for Young Singers* (a publication of NATS), and, as a nationally recognized expert on teaching beginning vocal study, has been featured in many speaking engagements and presentations on the subject.

CONTENTS

4   L'AMOUR DE MOI (Love of My Heart)   15th Century

10   BLOW, BLOW, THOU WINTER WIND   Thomas Arne

12   BLOW, YE WINDS   sea chantey, arranged by Celius Dougherty

18   BOIS EPAIS (Sombre Woods)   Jean-Baptise Lully

7   BRIGHT IS THE RING OF WORDS   Ralph Vaughan Williams

22   BUILD THEE MORE STATELY MANSIONS   Mark Andrews

26   DEEP RIVER   Spiritual, arranged by Harry T. Burleigh

28   DOWN HARLEY STREET   Charles Kingsford

30   DU BIST WIE EINE BLUME (Thou Art Lovely As a Flower)   Franz Liszt

32   DU BIST WIE EINE BLUME (Thou Art Lovely As a Flower)   Robert Schumann

34   EIN TON (What Sound is That?)   Peter Cornelius

37   ELDORADO   Richard H. Walthew

40   THE FIRST CONCERT   Mana-Zucca

46   GIVE A MAN A HORSE HE CAN RIDE   Geoffrey O'Hara

50   GOD IS MY SHEPHERD   Antonin Dvořák

52   THE HEART WORSHIPS   Gustav Holst

58   I WONDER AS I WANDER   John Jacob Niles

55   IN EINEM KÜHLEN GRUNDE (Mill of the Valley)   German Folksong

62   JESUS, FOUNT OF CONSOLATION   J. S. Bach

64   DIE KÖNIGE (The Kings)   Peter Cornelius

70   LE MIROIR (The Mirror)   Gustave Ferrari

72   O'ER THE HILLS   Francis Hopkinson

67   OS TORMENTOS DE AMOR (The Torments of Love)   arranged by Edward Kilenyi

78   PILGRIM'S SONG   Pytor Tchaikovsky

84   PRETTY AS A PICTURE   Victor Herbert

88   THE PRETTY CREATURE   Stephen Storace, arranged by H. Lane Wilson

94   THE ROADSIDE FIRE   Ralph Vaughan Williams

99   ROLLING DOWN TO RIO   Edward German

112   SEA FEVER   Mark Andrews

104   THE SLIGHTED SWAIN   English, arranged by H. Lane Wilson

108   THE SONG OF MOMUS TO MARS   William Boyce

120   TOGLIETEMI LA VITA ANCOR (Take Away My Life)   Alessandro Scarlatti

122   VERRATHENE LIEBE (Love's Secret Lost)   Robert Schumann

124   WAS IST SYLVIA? (Who Is Sylvia?)   Franz Schubert

117   DIE WETTERFAHNE (The Weathervane)   Franz Schubert

L'AMOUR DE MOI
(Love of My Heart)

English version by
Lorraine Noel Finley

15th Century
piano accompaniment
adapted from that of
Julien Tiersot

sant, Il est gar - ni de tou - tes flours.
stay, Bright-ly a-dorned by ev - 'ry flow'r.

ben legato

Hé - las! il n'est si dou - ce
Noth - ing more plain - tive ev - er

cho - - se Que de ce doux ros-si - gno-
sound - - ed Than lit-tle night - in-gales____ in

let Qui chan-te au soir,____ au ma - ti - net: Quand il est
spring:— All through the night____ till dawn,____ they sing; They rest when

BRIGHT IS THE RING OF WORDS

Robert Louis Stevenson

Ralph Vaughan Williams

Af - ter the sing - er is dead And the mak - er bur - ied.......... Low as the sing - er lies In the field of heath - er, Songs of his fash - ion bring The swains to - geth - er.

BLOW, BLOW, THOU WINTER WIND

from *As You Like It*
by William Shakespeare

Thomas Arne

In moderate time

1. Blow, blow, thou win-ter wind, ___ Thou art ___ not ___ so un - kind, ___ thou
2. Freeze, freeze, thou bit-ter sky, ___ Thou dost ___ not ___ bite so nigh, ___ thou

art not so un - kind As man's in - gra - - ti - tude. Thy
dost not bite so nigh As ben - e - fits _____ for - got. Tho'

BLOW, YE WINDS

sea chantey
arranged by
Celius Dougherty

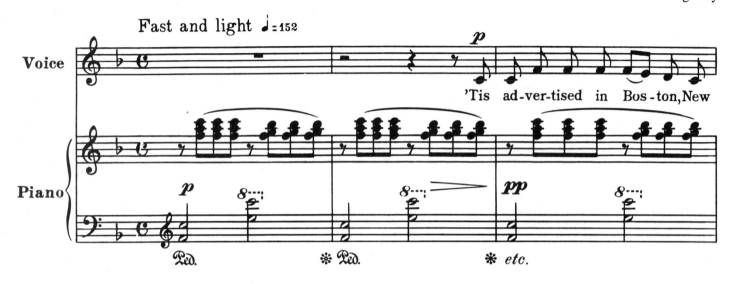

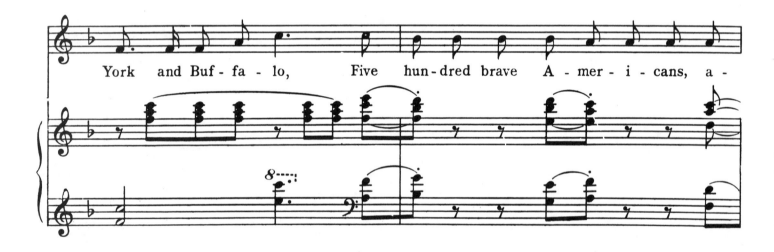

'Tis ad-ver-tised in Bos-ton, New York and Buf-fa-lo, Five hun-dred brave A-mer-i-cans, a-

whal-ing for to go,— sing-ing, Blow, ye winds in the morn — ing.

14

Blow, ye winds in the morn - ing, blow, ye winds, heigh - o.

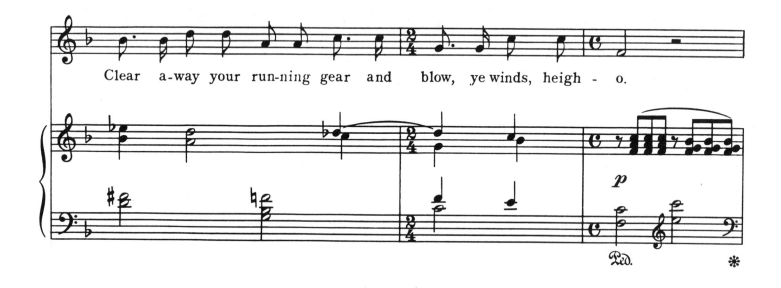

Clear a-way your run-ning gear and blow, ye winds, heigh - o.

It's now we're out to sea, boys, the wind comes on to blow. One

half the watch is sick on deck, the oth-er half be-low, sing-ing,

Blow, ye winds in the morn-ing, blow, ye winds, heigh-o.

Clear a-way your run-ning gear and blow, ye winds, heigh-o.

But now our trip is o - ver and we don't give a damn. We'll

bend on all our stu'n - sails and sail for Yan - kee land, sing - ing,

Blow, ye winds in the morn - ing, blow, ye winds, heigh - o.

Clear a-way your run-ning gear and blow, ye winds, heigh - o.

Blow, ye winds in the morn- ing,

soft but clear

in tempo

blow, ye winds, heigh-o.

BOIS ÉPAIS
(Sombre Woods)

Jean-Baptise Lully

Largo

mp

Bois é - pais re - dou - ble ton
Som - bre woods, ye glades dark and

om - bre, Tu ne sau - rais être as - sez
lone - ly, Where mid - night gloom ___ en - ters

Printed in the USA by G. Schirmer, Inc.

BUILD THEE MORE STATELY MANSIONS

Oliver Wendell Holmes

Mark Andrews

man-sions, O my soul,— more state-ly— man-sions, O——— my soul!—

Leave thy low-vault-ed past, leave thy low-vault-ed past, Let each new

tem - ple, no - bler than the last, Shut thee from heav - en with a

dome more vast,— Till thou at length art free, till thou at length art free,

24

DEEP RIVER

Spiritual,
arranged by Harry T. Burleigh

Deep _____ riv - er, Lord, I want to cross o - ver in - to camp - ground.

Oh, don't you want _ to go _____ to that gos - pel _____ feast, ___ That

prom - is'd land ___ where all _____ is peace? Oh

deep _____ riv - er, Lord, I want to cross o - ver in - to camp - ground. ___

DOWN HARLEY STREET

Benjamin Musser

Charles Kingsford

*Melody of final two measures may be whistled.

DU BIST WIE EINE BLUME

(Thou Art Lovely As a Flower)

Heinrich Heine
translation by Charles Fonteyn Manney

Franz Liszt

sotto voce

Mir ist als ob ich die
My hands, in ten - der de -

dolcissimo

Hän - de auf's Haupt dir le - gen sollt',
vo - tion, I'd rest up - on thy hair,

be - tend, dass dich Gott er - hal - te so rein und
Pray - ing, the dear God to keep thee So pure and

schön und hold.
sweet and fair.

DU BIST WIE EINE BLUME

(Thou Art Lovely As a Flower)

Heinrich Heine
translation by Charles Fonteyn Manney

Robert Schumann

EIN TON
(What Sound is That?)

text by the composer
translation by J. Ahrem

Peter Cornelius

Un poco agitato.

Mir klingt ein Ton so wun - der -
What sound is that so rich and

bar in Herz und Sin - nen im - mer - dar.
clear? It thrills my heart, it fills my ear;

Ist es der Hauch, der dir ent - schwebt, als ein - mal
Be - lov - ed one, and can it be Thy last fond

Printed in the USA by G. Schirmer, Inc.

noch dein Mund ge - bebt?_____ ist es des
sigh sent forth to me?_____ Was it the

cresc.

Glöckleins trü - ber Klang, der dir ge - folgt den Weg ent - lang?
bell in yon - der tow'r Which told me of thy last sad hour?

cresc.

Mir klingt der Ton so voll so rein, als schlöss er
And yet a - gain that sound I hear, As if thy

p

cresc.

dei - ne See - le ein,_____
soul still lin - gered near_____

fp dim.

pp

als stie - gest lie - bend nie - der du und sän - gest
To soothe my an - guish, calm my grief, And give my

mei - nen Schmerz in Ruh! _____
wound-ed heart re - lief. _____

ELDORADO

Edgar Allen Poe

Richard H. Walthew

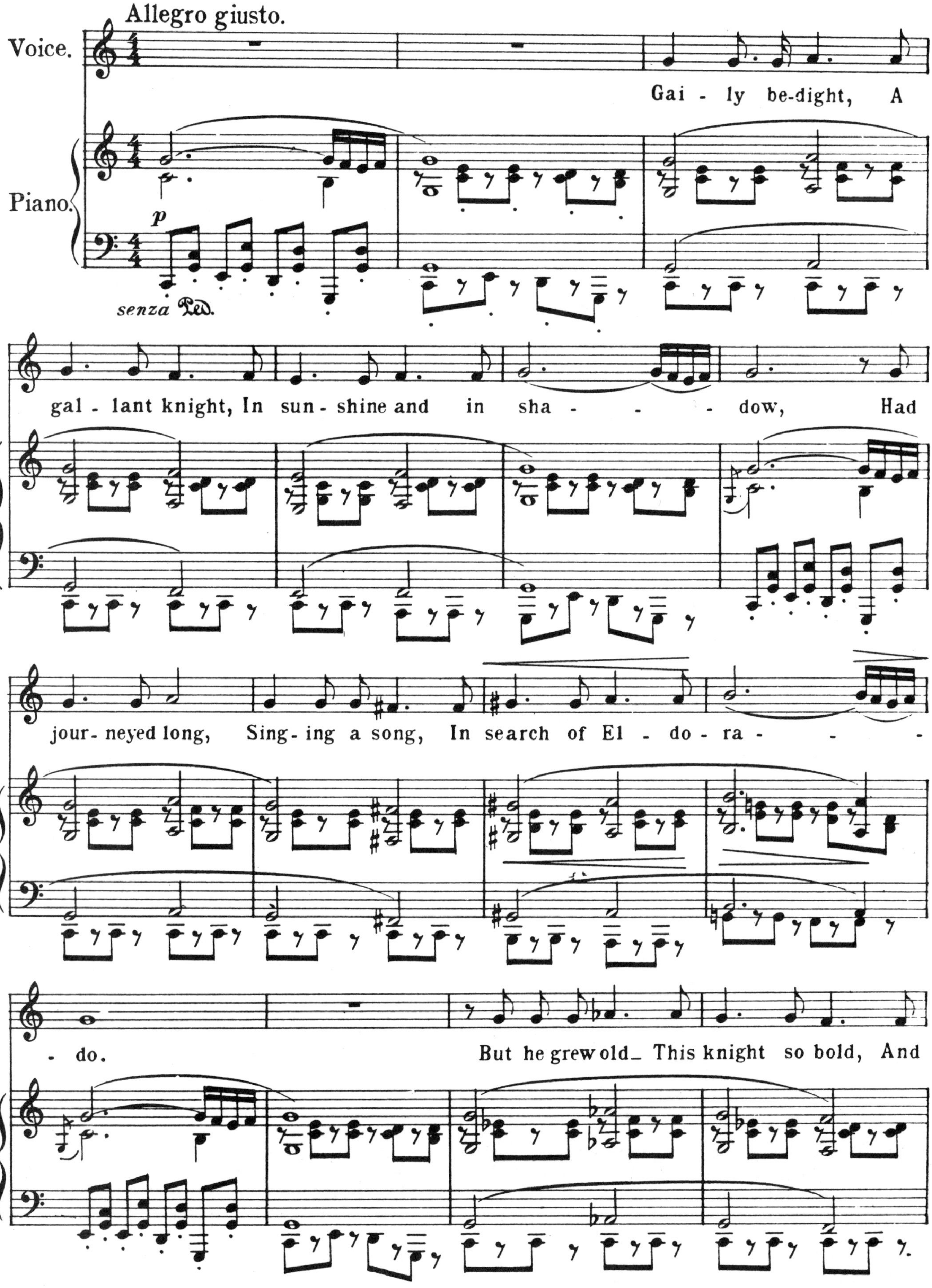

Allegro giusto.
Voice.
Piano.
p
senza Ped.
Gai - ly be-dight, A
gal - lant knight, In sun - shine and in sha - - - dow, Had
jour - neyed long, Sing - ing a song, In search of El - do - ra - - -
- do. But he grew old_ This knight so bold, And

Printed in the USA by G. Schirmer, Inc.

o'er his heart a sha - - - - dow Fell,........

.... as he found No spot of ground That looked like El - do -

- ra - - - do.......................

And as his strength Failed him at length, He met a pil - grim

sha - - dow— "Sha-dow," said he, "Where can it be— This

THE FIRST CONCERT

Sylvia Golden

Mana-Zucca

And be - fore I knew it, I whist - led a - long. Then ma poked me, an' the ush - er came, And what ev - er was wrong ___ I got the blame. All was still as he held on one note, And

speak

quick as that, somethin' tickled my throat, And I coughed and coughed till my face got blue, And Ma

cough and choke and sputter

o - ver the keys his fin - gers ran fast While I

won - dered and won - dered how long it would last. Oh! I

sneezed and I coughed and I tried hold - ing back, But my

breaf got so short,— then an - oth - er at - tack! From a-

cough and sputter

45

GIVE A MAN A HORSE HE CAN RIDE

James Thomson

Geoffrey O'Hara

sea nor shore shall fail!___ Give a man a horse he can ride,___ Give a

man a boat he can sail,___ And his rank and wealth, his strength and health, On

sea nor shore___ shall fail!___ Give a

man a pipe he can smoke,___ Give a man a book he can read___ And his

molto rit. e marcato

thee, ___ And his heart is great, with the pulse of Fate, At home, on land, on

molto rit. e marcato

a tempo

sea, ___ Give a man a girl he can love, ___ As I, my love, love

a tempo

gradually slower and broader to finish

thee, ___ And his heart is great with the pulse of Fate, At home, on ___

gradually slower and broader to finish

land ___ on sea!

ff vivace

sfz   *sfz*   *sfz*

GOD IS MY SHEPHERD

paraphrase of Psalm 23

Antonin Dvorák
(from the Biblical Songs)

THE HEART WORSHIPS

Alice M. Buckton

Gustav Holst

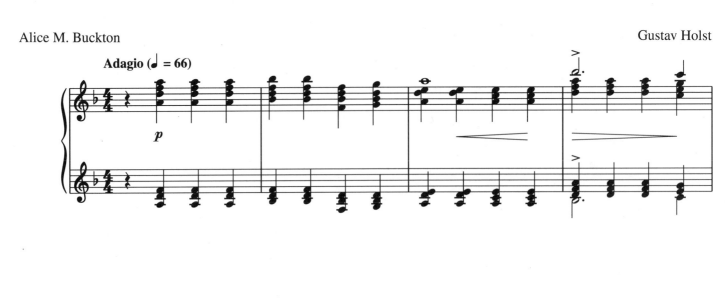

Si - lence in Heav'n –

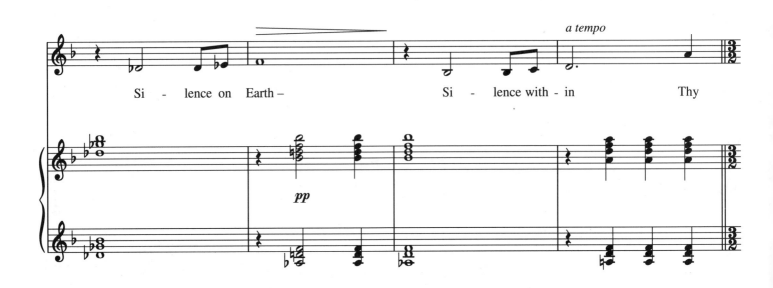

Si - lence on Earth –   Si - lence with - in   Thy

touch   to   win;   Si - lence in

Heav'n –   Si - lence on Earth –   Si - lence with –

in!

rall.   pp

IN EINEM KÜHLEN GRUNDE

(Mill of the Valley)

Joseph, Freiherr von Eichendorff

German Folksong

Allegretto.

In ei - nem küh - len Grun - de, da geht ein Müh - len -
On yon - der fleet - ing riv - er There turns a bus - y

rad, _____ mein Lieb - chen ist __ ver - schwun - den, __ das
wheel, _____ My Love has fled; __ ah! sor - - row, __ Which

dort ge - woh - net hat, _____ mein Lieb - chen ist __ ver -
time can nev - er heal, _____ My Love, ah! bit - ter

schwun - den __ das dort ge - woh - net hat
sor - - row, __ Which time can nev - er heal.

Printed in the USA by G. Schirmer, Inc.

Sie hat mir Treu' ver-spro- chen, gab mir ein'n Ring da-
She gave as true - love to- -ken A beau - teous ring of

bei, _____ sie hat die Treu'__ ge-bro- -chen das
gold. _____ The ring is long__ since brok- -en, Her

Ring - lein brach ent - zwei, _____ sie hat__ die Treu' ge-
love is dead and cold, _____ Her true__ love, which she

bro- -chen, das Ring - lein brach ent - zwei. Hör'
prom- -ised, Is past, is dead, and cold. And

I WONDER AS I WANDER

Collected by
John Jacob Niles

Appalachian Carol
adapted and arranged
by John Jacob Niles

When Ma - ry birthed Je - sus, 'twas in a cow's stall, With

wise men and farm-ers and shep-herds and all. But high from God's heav-en a

star's light did fall, And the prom - ise of a - ges it then did re - call.

JESUS, FOUNT OF CONSOLATION

from the *Schmelli Gesangbuch*

translation by Troutbeck

J. S. Bach

1. Je - sus, Fount of con - so - la - tion, Who through Death has wrought sal - va - tion, Who through heaven - ly love and
2. He for Man has brave - ly striv - en, Power from Death and Hell has riv - en Foes that can - not harm us

Printed in the USA by G. Schirmer, Inc.

might,   Death - - less life ____ has brought to ____
more,   Fierce - - ly though ____ they rage to and ____

light,   He ____ is held of ____ Death no ____
roar.   Zi - - on right - ly ____ then re - -

long - er,   He ____ than Death it - - self ____ is
joi - ces: Sing ____ we all, with ____ hearts ____ and

strong - er. Hal - le - lu - jah! ____ Hal - le - lu - jah!
voi - ces,   Hal - le - lu - jah! ____ Hal - le - lu - jah!

DIE KÖNIGE
(The Kings)

text by the composer
revised by Henry Clough-Leighter

Peter Cornelius

And bright - ly shi - neth the guid - ing star; Un - to the man - ger the
Und hell er - glän - zet des Ster - nes Schein; zum Stal - le ge - hen die

kings re - pair; With rap - ture fill'd, on the Boy they_ gaze, And bow be -
Kön' - ge ein; das Knäb - lein schau - en sie won - nig - lich, an - be - tend

fore_ Him in_ joy and praise. With gold and myrrh and in - cense
nei - gen die_ Kön' - ge_ sich; sie brin - gen Weih - rauch, Myr - rhen und

sweet, They bring the_ Ho - ly Boy an of - f'ring meet.___
Gold zum O - pfer dar_____ dem Knäb - lein_ hold.___

OS TORMENTOS DE AMOR
(The Torments of Love)

Brazilian Folksong,
arranged by Edward Kilenyi

68

69

LE MIROIR
(The Mirror)

Haraucourt
translation by Lorraine Noel Finley

Gustave Ferrari

roir qui lui - sait comme un mor - ceau des ___ cieux.
mir - ror that shone as clear as lam - bent ___ skies.

A - lors, seul, je me suis in - cli -
A - lone there, as I leaned toward these

né vers ces cho - ses, Et j'ai pi - eu - se - ment, de mes deux lè - vres clo -
trea - sures, e - lat - ed, With rev - er - ence I saw the mir - ror all trans - lat- -

ses, Bai - sé sur le mi - roir la pla - ce de vos yeux. _____
ed, And then I kissed the place re - flect - ing your dear eyes. _____

O'ER THE HILLS

Francis Hopkinson

PILGRIM'S SONG

Paul England

Pytor Il'yich Tchaikovsky

My bless-ing fall on this fair world, On mountain, valley, for-est,

to   my___ heart!

PRETTY AS A PICTURE

from *Sweethearts*

Robert B. Smith

Victor Herbert

Moderato

sempre assai rubato

When Na-ture draws the pic-ture true, The wo-man adds a line or two; She steals the col-or

scheme Of peach-es mixed with cream, When Na-ture's done the best she could, The

eye-brows arched as eye-brows should; Like-wise the hair is made_____ A

poco rit.   *poco animato*

most be-witch-ing shade;_____ No paint-ing's done with so much care, No

won - der all the men declare: "She's pret - ty as a pic - ture,

Bloom-ing as a rose, Grace in ev - 'ry move - ment, Charm in ev - 'ry

pose." Ha! ha! O clev-er lit - tle wo-man, We all un-der-stand That

Na-ture can - not make you What you can do by hand

THE PRETTY CREATURE

Stephen Storace,
arranged by H. Lane Wilson

But

then her wick-ed, charm-ing eyes, When she looks up, show

kind sur-prise; I, like an awk-ward, fool-ish clown,

I, like an awk-ward, fool-ish clown, When she looks up, must

THE ROADSIDE FIRE

Robert Louis Stevenson

Ralph Vaughan Williams

95

ROLLING DOWN TO RIO

Rudyard Kipling

Edward German

Allegro marcato (♩ = 112)

I've never sailed the A - ma - zon, I've nev - er reached Bra - zil; But the

"Don" and the "Mag - da - le - na," They can go there when they will! Ah!

love to roll to Ri - o some - day be - fore I'm old! to

roll, _____ I'd

love to roll to Ri - o some - day be - fore I'm

old. _____

THE SLIGHTED SWAIN

17th century English,
arranged by H. Lane Wilson

Tempo di Minuetto

THE SONG OF MOMUS TO MARS

John Dryden
from "Secular Masque"

William Boyce

Printed in the USA by G. Schirmer, Inc.

kept a - wake by Thee; bet - ter the World were fast a - sleep than

kept a - wake by Thee, bet - ter fast a - sleep than

kept a - wake by Thee.

Thy

The

SEA FEVER

John Masefield

Mark Andrews

wheel's kick, and the wind's song and the white sail's shak-ing, A gray mist on the

sea's face and a gray_____ dawn break-ing.

I must go down to the seas a-gain, for the call of the run-ning

slower

must go down to the seas a - gain, to the va - grant gyp - sy

p slower

Tempo I°

life,_____ To the gull's way and the whale's way where the wind's like a whet-ted

knife;_____ And all I ask is a mer-ry yarn from a laugh-ing fel - low-

DIE WETTERFAHNE
(The Weathervane)

Wilhelm Müller

English translation by Theodore Baker

Franz Schubert

Molto vivace.

PIANO.

Now with the vane the wind is toy-ing, That on—my sweetheart's
Der Wind spielt mit— der Wet-ter-fah-ne auf mei-nes schö-nen

house-top veers! It seems to me as if 'twere joy-ing In mock-'ry
Lieb-chens Haus. Da dacht' ich schon in meinem Wahne: sie pfiff—den

at—my sighs and tears.— Had I but notic'd it ere— I en-ter'd, The
ar-men Flücht-ling aus.— Er hätt' es e-her be-mer-ken sol-len des

118

TOGLIETEMI LA VITA ANCOR

(Take Away My Life)

Take away my life, cruel heavens,
If you wish to steal my heart.
Deny me the light of day, ruthless stars,
If you are happy with my sorrow.

Alessandro Scarlatti

Printed in the USA by G. Schirmer, Inc.

VERRATHENE LIEBE
(Love's Secret Lost)

Adelbert von Chamisso
translation by Frederic Field Bullard

Robert Schumann